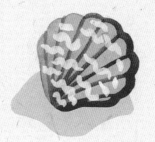

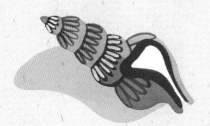
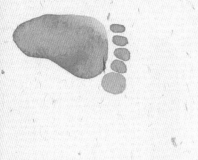

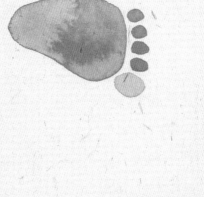

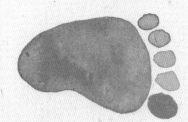
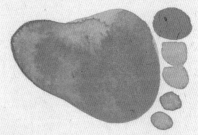

For Vince Reid, 1935–2001, one of the youngest
passengers to have made that Windrush journey
JA

For the Windrush Generation
SB

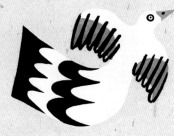

First US edition 2023
First published by Walker Books Ltd. (UK) 2022

Library of Congress Catalog Card Number 2022908131
ISBN 978-1-5362-2853-3

23 24 25 26 27 28 APS 10 9 8 7 6 5 4 3 2 1

Printed in Humen, Dongguan, China

This book was typeset in Archer.
The illustrations were done in gouache and pen.

Candlewick Press
99 Dover Street
Somerville, Massachusetts 02144

www.candlewick.com

WINDRUSH CHILD

THE TALE OF A CARIBBEAN CHILD
WHO FACED A NEW HORIZON

John Agard

illustrated by
Sophie Bass

CANDLEWICK PRESS

Behind you

Windrush child

palm trees wave goodbye

above you
Windrush child
seabirds asking why

around you

Windrush child

blue water rolling by

beside you
Windrush child
your Windrush mom and dad

think of mango mornings
and storytime verandas

and new beginnings

doors closing and opening

will things turn out right?

At least the ship will arrive

in midsummer light

and you Windrush child

think of Grandmother

telling you don't forget to write

and with one last hug

walk good walk good

and the sea's wheel carries on spinning

and from that place England

you tell her in a letter

of your Windrush adventure

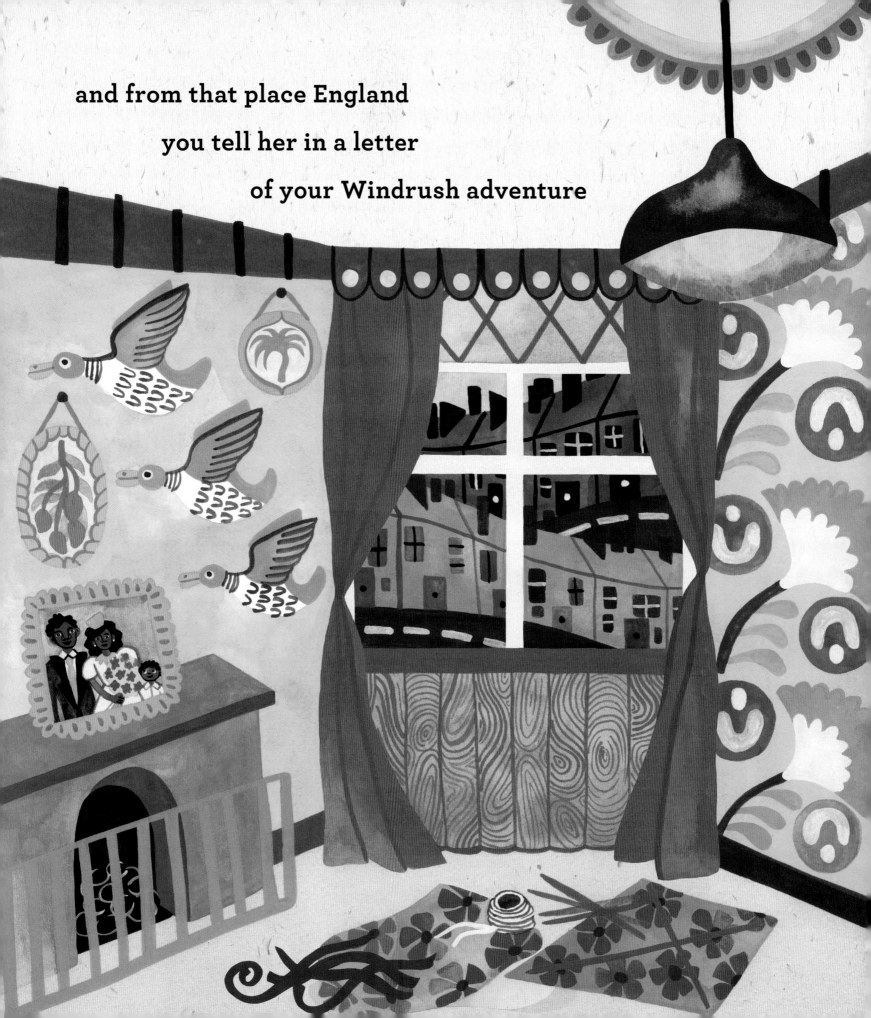

stepping in a big ship

not knowing how long the journey

or that you're stepping into history

bringing your Caribbean eye

to another horizon

Grandmother's words your shining beacon

learning how to fly

the kite of your dreams

in an English sky

Windrush child

walking good walking good

in a mind-opening

meeting of snow and sun

A Note from the Author

On June 22, 1948, the ship *Empire Windrush* arrived at Tilbury Docks, England. On board were hundreds of men, women, and children from across the Caribbean who had paid the fee of £28 10s. (about $1,440 today) to sail to Britain. Among them were some famous faces, including the calypso musician Lord Kitchener, the jazz singer Mona Baptiste, and Sam King, who would go on to be elected mayor of the London Borough of Southwark. Also on the ship were Royal Air Force servicemen who had fought during World War II, other British adults returning from the Caribbean, and a group of Polish refugees.

Between 1948 and 1971, thousands of adults and children followed in their footsteps. These people have been called the Windrush Generation. Many decided to move to Britain as they hoped to make a new life. They were drawn by the promise of good jobs and opportunity from the British government, which had asked people in the Caribbean to help rebuild the country after the damage caused by the war. Some were returning to Britain having lived there before or having fought for Britain during the war. Others came because it was an adventure. While some planned to stay in Britain permanently, others knew they wanted to return to the Caribbean one day.

When they arrived in Britain, they discovered a country that was different from their Caribbean home. It was sometimes hard to find jobs or even a safe place to live. But despite many challenges, including racism, they went on to build strong communities: friends were made, stories shared, and unfairness challenged. Caribbean culture has had a powerful and positive impact on British culture, and Britain is a much better place because of the Windrush Generation.

John Agard is a poet, playwright, and short story writer who grew up in Guyana, where his love of language was sparked by listening to cricket commentaries on the radio. He has won many prizes, including a CLPE Poetry Award, the Queen's Medal for Poetry, and a BookTrust Lifetime Achievement Award. He has been a writer in residence at the BBC; the Southbank Centre, in London; and the National Maritime Museum, in London. He tours widely, giving performances and speaking to students. John Agard lives in England.

Sophie Bass draws inspiration from her mixed British and Trinidadian heritage and from music, social justice, mythology, and symbolism. She works by hand, employing traditional techniques with gouache and pen, to create contemporary images characterized by strong figures, vivid colors, and a distinctive style. Sophie Bass lives and works in London.